Read-Along
STORYBOOK AND CD

It's tough being a toy. Oh, sure, it looks like fun from the outside. But there's a lot more to it than that. Do you want to hear more about it? Read along with me in your book. You will know it's time to turn the page when you hear this sound. . . . Let's begin now.

For information address Disney Press, 1200 Grand Central Avenue, Glendale, California 91201.

Printed in the United States of America

First Paperback Edition, May 2019   10 9 8 7 6 5 4 3 2 1

ISBN 978-1-368-04282-6   FAC-038091-19081

Library of Congress Control Number: 2018964443

Visit www.disneybooks.com

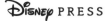

Disney PRESS
Los Angeles • New York

Logo Applies to Text Stock Only

Play Track 1 on your CD now!

Andy was a young boy with a big imagination. He loved playing with all his toys, but his favorite was a cowboy doll named Sheriff Woody. And when no one was around, Andy's toys came to life!

One very special day, Andy left Woody on his bed while he went downstairs with his baby sister.

Once the kids were gone, Woody looked around and stood up. "Okay, everybody. Coast is clear!" Andy's family was moving soon, and Woody was trying to keep the toys organized.

Woody called the toys to order. "Okay. Ah . . . oh, yes, one minor note here . . . Andy's birthday party has been moved to today."

The toys gasped. Andy would be getting new toys sooner than they expected!

Suddenly, Hamm the piggy bank called out. "Birthday guests at three o'clock!" The toys ran to the window. Even though Woody was trying to keep them calm, they were getting scared.

Woody sent a group of Green Army Men to keep an eye out for new toys. The Green Army Men hid in a plant and told Woody about each present as it was opened.

Woody and the others nervously listened to the Green Army Men's reports. There was a surprise gift. "It's a huge package. Oh, wha—It's . . . It's a—"

In all the excitement, Rex the dinosaur bumped into the speaker, and the batteries fell out. Moments later, Andy and his friends raced upstairs to his room.

The kids played with the new toy and then ran back downstairs for birthday cake.

Woody peeked at the cool new toy. His name was Buzz Lightyear.

The cowboy approached Buzz. "There has been a bit of a mix-up. This is my spot, see, the bed here."

The other toys crowded around the new toy.

Buzz pressed a button, and wings popped out from his back! All the toys were impressed—except for Woody. "These are plastic. He can't fly!"

"Yes, I can. Stand back, everyone. To infinity, and beyond!" Buzz leaped off the bed, bounced off some toys, and landed in front of Woody. All the toys cheered!

Woody couldn't believe it. "Well, in a couple of days, everything will be just the way it was. They'll see. I'm still Andy's favorite toy."

Woody was jealous of Andy playing with Buzz so much. One day, Woody was trying to make sure Andy chose him over Buzz. But he accidentally knocked Buzz out of the window!

Mr. Potato Head saw it all and confronted Woody. "Couldn't handle Buzz cutting in on your playtime, could you, Woody?"

"No, no! Wait, wait, wait! I can explain everything."

Just then, Andy picked up Woody and carried him out to the van. Buzz, who had landed in a nearby bush, raced after the van and jumped onto the bumper.

The van pulled into a gas station, and Andy got out, leaving Woody on the backseat. Woody tried to explain to Buzz that he really was a toy, but Buzz thought he was a real space ranger with a mission to complete. The two of them got into a big fight and fell out of the van. Then the van drove away!

As Buzz walked off, a Pizza Planet delivery truck pulled into the gas station. Woody convinced Buzz that the truck could help get him back to his planet.

Soon the two toys arrived at Pizza Planet. Buzz looked around in amazement. "What . . . the spaceport!"

Buzz jumped inside a game shaped like a rocket. He met a group of squeeze-toy aliens. "I am Buzz Lightyear. Who's in charge here?"

The aliens pointed up at a crane. "The claw is our master."

Woody followed Buzz into the claw game, but he was scared when he saw who was playing. It was Sid, Andy's mean neighbor who destroyed toys for fun. Sid grabbed Woody and Buzz and took both of them home.

Sid was excited that he'd found new toys to destroy. He left them in his room. Woody knew they had to escape, but the door was locked.

Woody heard a noise. He turned and saw a doll's head looking out from under the bed. Woody smiled. "Hi there, little fella. Come out here. Do you know a way out of here?"

The head came toward Woody, but it had a creepy, spiderlike body. Then the doll was joined by other mutant toys. Woody was frightened.

Buzz pushed a button on his chest. "Mayday! Mayday! Come in, Star Command! Send reinforcements!"

But instead of attacking, the mutant toys crept back out of sight.

NOT A FLYING TOY

The next morning, Sid woke up and went downstairs without locking the door behind him. Woody and Buzz quickly left the room.

A voice rang out. "Calling Buzz Lightyear! This is Star Command!" The voice was coming from a TV commercial advertising Buzz Lightyear toys. Buzz realized Woody had been right all along. He *was* just a toy.

Stunned, Buzz went to the top of the stairs. He opened his wings and jumped, trying to fly. Instead, he crashed to the floor, and one of his plastic arms popped off.

Woody found the one-armed Buzz. "Look at me. I can't even
fly out of a window."

Woody smiled. "Out the window . . . Buzz, you're a genius!"

The cowboy ran to Sid's window, which faced Andy's room.
He tried to get the attention of his friends. "Hey, guys! Guys!"

Woody waved Buzz's arm to show the other toys that Buzz was okay. But he held it too high. The others saw that it had been broken off. They thought Woody had hurt Buzz!

As they hurried away from the window, Woody called out. "You've got to help us, please! You don't know what it's like over here!"

All of a sudden, Sid's toys grabbed Buzz's arm. They surrounded Buzz before Woody could stop them.

When they backed away, Buzz's arm was back in place! Woody was amazed. "Hey . . . hey, they fixed you!"

Just then, Sid came into the room
holding a giant rocket. "What am I
gonna blow? Man . . . hey, where's
that wimpy cowboy doll?"

Woody was hiding, so
Sid taped the rocket onto
Buzz. "Yes! To infinity
and beyond!"

Then it started to
rain. Sid would have to
wait until the next day.

While Sid slept, Woody called to Buzz for help. Buzz wouldn't move. "I'm just a toy."

Woody glared at him. "Look, over in that house is a kid who thinks you are the greatest, and it's not because you're a space ranger, pal. It's because you're a toy. You are his toy!"

All of a sudden, Sid's alarm clock rang. He jumped out of bed, grabbed Buzz, and ran outside!

Woody convinced Sid's toys to help him save Buzz. They went outside. Sid spotted Woody in the grass and picked him up. Just then, all of Sid's toys surrounded them. Woody looked right at Sid. "From now on, you must take good care of your toys. Because if you don't, we'll find out, Sid."

Woody's plan worked! Sid was scared. He ran into the house, screaming.

As Woody rushed to help Buzz, a car horn honked. Next door, Andy's family and their moving truck were leaving. Buzz and Woody raced after the truck.

Buzz grabbed a loose strap hanging from the back of the truck and climbed on board. Woody was right behind him, but Sid's dog Scud ran after them. Scud grabbed Woody with his teeth. Buzz jumped off the truck to save Woody, but Scud held on to Buzz!

Now it was up to Woody to save Buzz.

Woody opened the back of the truck and found Andy's toys. He pushed RC the remote-controlled car onto the street and started driving it toward Buzz. But Mr. Potato Head thought Woody was trying to get rid of other toys, and pushed him off the truck!

RC Car picked up Buzz and Woody and raced back to the truck.

Just as Slinky Dog was about to grab them, RC Car's batteries ran out!

Luckily, Woody and Buzz had an idea. The cowboy lit the fuse on Buzz's rocket. The toys shot straight into the air. They dropped RC Car safely into the back of the truck.

Buzz popped open his wings, setting the rocket free before it could explode.

Woody was thrilled. "Hey, Buzz, you're flying!"

The two of them glided over the van where Andy was. They fell through the open sunroof and into a box. When Andy turned around, he let out a happy yell.

"Hey! Wow! Woody! Buzz!" He had missed his two favorite toys.

That Christmas, Andy was opening his presents, and the toys were listening in. Woody smiled. "Buzz Lightyear, you are not worried, are you?"

"Me? No! No. No, no, no, no. Are you?"

"Now, Buzz, what could Andy possibly get that is worse than you?"

It was a puppy! The toys looked at each other. Here came their next adventure.

Read-Along
STORYBOOK AND CD

Buzz Lightyear and Woody are not only Andy's favorite
toys, they are also best friends. To find out what
happens when they get separated, read along with me
in your book. You will know it's time to turn the page
when you hear this sound. . . . Let's begin now.

Play
Track 2
on your
CD now!

DISNEP PRESS
Los Angeles • New York

Woody the cowboy doll was excited. Soon he was going to Cowboy Camp with Andy.

While Woody got ready, Rex the dinosaur watched a TV commercial for Al's Toy Barn.

Hamm the piggy bank saw it, too. "I despise that chicken."

Just then Andy burst into the room. As he played with his toys, Andy tore Woody's arm. "Oh, no!"

Andy decided to leave Woody at home. So Andy's mom put the cowboy on a shelf next to Wheezy, a penguin toy with a broken squeaker.

Wheezy had been sitting on the shelf for ages. After all, no one wanted to play with a broken toy. The toys watched Andy ride away.

A while later, Wheezy pointed out the window. "We're all just one stitch away from here . . . to there." Outside, Andy's mom was setting up a yard sale.

Soon Andy's mom took Wheezy out to the sale.

Woody whistled for Andy's dog, Buster, and strapped Wheezy onto him, but Woody slipped off.

A man at the yard sale saw Woody and became very excited.
"I found him! I found him!" When Andy's mom refused to sell
Woody, the man stole him!

Buzz tried to save his friend, but the man drove away. Luckily,
Buzz saw his license plate. It read LZTYBRN.

Back in Andy's room, Buzz punched the letters from the license plate into Mr. Spell to try and figure out what they stood for. "Lousy-Try-Brian?"

"Toy, toy, toy . . . hold on!"

"Al's Toy Barn." The man from the TV commercial had taken Woody! The toys came up with a plan to rescue their friend.

Al took Woody to his apartment, then left.

Woody looked around. He needed to find a way to escape. He was trying to open an air vent when he saw a toy horse named Bullseye, a cowgirl toy named Jessie, and a gold prospector called Stinky Pete.

Jessie seemed thrilled to see him. "It *is* you!"

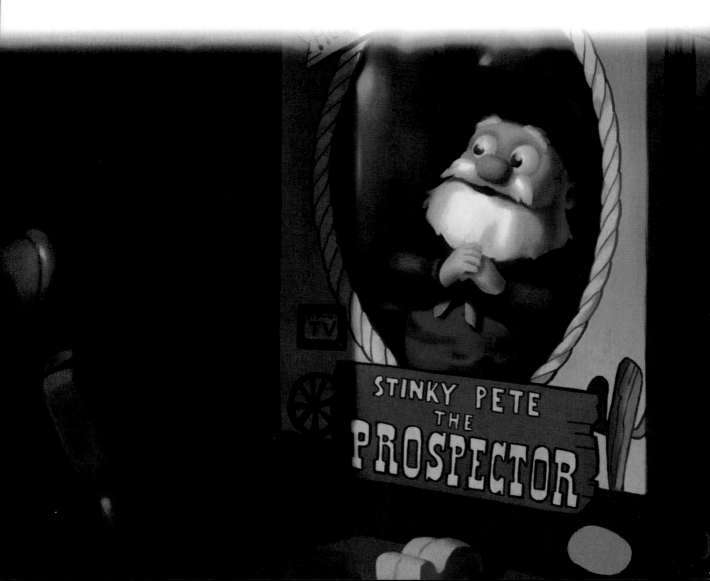

Jessie and Bullseye showed Woody a rerun of a 1950s TV show called *Woody's Roundup*. A character who looked just like Woody was the star! Now that Woody was there, Al had a complete set of *Woody's Roundup* toys to sell to a museum in Japan.

Woody frowned. "Japan? No, no, no, no, no, no, no! I can't go to Japan. I've got to get back home to my owner, Andy."

Jessie got mad. Without Woody, she'd have to go into storage.

The next morning, Buzz and the other toys arrived across the street from Al's Toy Barn. They had left Andy's house the night before. Disguising themselves with orange safety cones, the toys crossed the street. Tires squealed as cars stopped, but the toys got there safely.

Once they were inside Al's Toy Barn, Buzz set off down an aisle.
"Look for Al. We find Al, we find Woody." The toys split up.

Buzz found an entire aisle of new Buzz Lightyear toys. He accidentally awakened one of them.

The other Buzz thought he was a real space ranger. "You're in direct violation of Code 6404.5." He trapped Andy's Buzz inside a box. When the other toys arrived, they mistook New Buzz for their friend.

Back at Al's apartment, Woody had decided to return to Andy.

Then Jessie told him about Emily, the little girl who had been her owner. Emily had grown up and given Jessie away.

The Prospector looked at Woody. "Andy's growing up, and there's nothing you can do about it."

Woody decided to stay. "Who am I to break up the *Roundup* gang?"

By this time, New Buzz and the other toys had made it to Al's office. They hid in his bag, thinking it might get them closer to Woody.

Inside the store, Andy's Buzz had finally escaped. As he ran outside, Buzz knocked over a stack of boxes. Emperor Zurg, the toy that was Buzz Lightyear's archenemy in space, escaped.

The newly freed Zurg followed Buzz across the parking lot. "Destroy Buzz Lightyear. Destroy Buzz Lightyear."

Al left his bag in the car and went to his apartment. New Buzz found an air vent and pulled the toys up the elevator shaft using a line on his new utility belt. Then he had an idea. "What was I thinking? My antigravity servos!"

But since he was a toy, the antigravity servos wouldn't work. New Buzz let go of the wall, and the toys tumbled down the shaft.

Meanwhile, Andy's Buzz had arrived. He followed the toys.

New Buzz and the other toys finally made it to Al's apartment. They trapped Jessie and Bullseye and grabbed Woody. But Woody didn't want to leave.

Then Andy's Buzz arrived. He tried to convince Woody to come home. Woody wasn't so sure. "I can't abandon these guys."

"You are a toy!"

"I don't have a choice, Buzz. This is my only chance."

"To do what, Woody? Never be loved again? Some life."

Buzz and the other toys left.

Woody turned to the TV and saw a boy who looked like Andy. He looked at Andy's name on his boot and realized he'd made a mistake. Woody turned to the *Roundup* gang. "Hey, you guys, come with me!"

The Prospector screwed the vent shut. "Finally, my waiting has paid off, and no hand-me-down cowboy doll is going to mess it up for me now."

On the other side of the vent, New Buzz and Andy's toys watched.

Moments later, Al arrived. He packed Woody and the *Roundup* gang into a case and left for the airport.

Andy's toys and New Buzz jumped down onto an elevator. Zurg
was there! New Buzz battled Zurg while the other toys opened the
elevator ceiling panel.

Zurg aimed his ion blaster at New Buzz.

Rex turned away. "*Ahhh!* I can't look!" His tail knocked Zurg
down the elevator shaft!

The other toys had opened the elevator hatch, so Slinky stretched down as far as he could. Just as he was about to grab Woody, the Prospector pulled Woody back.

Al hurried outside and drove away.

The toys hopped into an empty Pizza Planet truck with three
Little Green Aliens. "Oooh. Strangers from the outside."
New Buzz stayed behind.
Buzz and the toys drove to the airport and snuck in.

Buzz found the case Woody was in and opened it. But the Prospector attacked Buzz.

Woody grabbed him. "Hey! No one does that to my friend!"

Buzz and Woody stunned him with a camera flash and tossed him into a backpack.

Woody and Bullseye had escaped from the case, but Jessie hadn't. The case was loaded onto the plane.

Buzz and Woody had to rescue her. They hopped on Bullseye and galloped toward the plane. "Ride like the wind, Bullseye!"

Woody managed to get on the plane and find Jessie. "C'mon, Jess. It's time to take you home." Woody twirled his pull string like a lasso and looped it around a bolt. The plane had started moving.

Woody and Jessie swung down toward the runway. Just then, the pull string unhooked!

Luckily, Buzz and Bullseye were galloping along the runway.
They caught Woody and Jessie, and everyone was safe! "Nice ropin',
cowboy."

Woody turned to the toys after the plane took off. "Let's go home."

Andy liked Jessie and Bullseye immediately. "New toys! Cool!"
When he left, Buzz turned to Woody. "You still worried?"
"About Andy? Nah. It'll be fun while it lasts."
"I'm proud of you, cowboy."
"Besides, when it all ends, I'll have old Buzz Lightyear to keep
me company . . . for infinity and beyond."

Disney · PIXAR

TOY STORY 3

Read-Along
STORYBOOK AND CD

Andy is almost ready to go to college. To
find out what happens to Buzz, Woody,
and the other toys, read along with me in
your book. You will know it's time to turn
the page when you hear this sound. . . .
Let's begin now.

**Play
Track 3
on your
CD now!**

Disney PRESS
Los Angeles • New York

For a long time, Woody the cowboy felt as if he
was the luckiest toy in the world. He belonged to
Andy, who loved him as much as anyone could.

For years, Andy played with Woody, Buzz,
Jessie, and all his other toys. Like all children,
though, Andy grew up.

One day, Woody told the other toys that Andy was going to college. "We all knew this day was coming."

Buzz Lightyear the space ranger tried to cheer them up. "Whatever happens, at least we'll all be together."

Andy packed Woody into a box to bring to college. He put his other toys in a bag to take up to the attic. But Andy's mom thought the bag was trash and took it outside.

Woody saw the mistake. He knew he had to save his friends. "Think, Woody! Think, think, think!"

Finally, Woody made it to the curb. He opened the bags, but all he found was garbage. Where had the toys gone?

Woody spotted the toys in the garage.

"It's under control, Woody. We have a plan!" Buzz and the other toys thought Andy didn't want them anymore. They had decided to get in a box that was being sent to Sunnyside Daycare.

Woody tried to explain. "He was putting you in the attic! I know it looks bad, but guys, you've got to believe me!"

Jessie the cowgirl wasn't convinced. "Andy's moving on, Woody. It's time we did the same."

Just then, the car doors closed. All the toys, including Woody, were on their way.

At Sunnyside, the toys were greeted by a bear named Lotso. "Well, hello there!" He showed them to the toddler classroom. "Here's where you folks will be staying."

The toys were excited to see so many children!

Rex the dinosaur couldn't wait for recess to end. "Why can't time go faster?"

Woody was frustrated. "You have a kid—Andy. Now I'm going home!" He marched away alone.

Woody snuck onto the roof. He found an old kite and tried to fly it back to Andy's house, but it crashed into a tree!

Just then, a little girl named Bonnie walked by. She thought Woody was lost, so she took him home.

In the toddler room, Buzz got the toys together. "Places, everyone!"
Then the kids came in. Playtime was awful! By the end, Rex's tail
was missing and Slinky Dog was all tangled up.

"Andy never played with us like that!"

Buzz went to Lotso to request a transfer.

"Those kids need *someone* to play with." Lotso told Buzz he could move, but the other toys had to stay. Buzz refused, so Lotso's crew pushed his reset button.

The space ranger forgot about his friends!

Meanwhile, Mrs. Potato Head discovered something. She could see what was happening at Andy's house with the eye she'd left behind. "I think he did mean to put us in the attic."

"Woody was telling the truth!" Slinky Dog and the other toys realized they had made a mistake.

Jessie took charge. "We gotta go home!"
Lotso and his gang walked in. "You ain't leavin' Sunnyside."
Jessie wasn't scared. "And who's gonna stop us?"

Buzz still didn't remember that Andy's toys were his friends. Following Lotso's orders, he trapped them. "Prisoners disabled, Commander Lotso!"

Jessie wondered how they would escape. "I miss Woody."

Woody was having a wonderful time at Bonnie's house. Still, he kept thinking about Andy. "He's leaving soon. I've got to get home."

Then Woody found out Bonnie's toys knew about Sunnyside Daycare.

They told Woody that Lotso had belonged to a girl named
Daisy. She had lost him, and by the time he found his way
back, Daisy had gotten a new toy bear. Since then, Lotso had
hated new toys.

"My friends are in there!" Woody had to save them—fast!

Woody snuck into Sunnyside Daycare in Bonnie's backpack. "We're busting out of here tonight!"

First the toys had to get Buzz back to normal. They trapped him in a bin.

"Open his back! There's a switch!"

The toys accidentally reset Buzz to Spanish mode. "C'mon, El Buzzo!" Woody led the toys to the playground. They snuck past Lotso's guard, a doll named Big Baby.

At last the toys made it through a chute that led outside. All they had to do was get across an open Dumpster.

Then Lotso appeared. "Well, well . . . Look who's back!" He tried to get Big Baby to stop them.

Lotso ended up inside the Dumpster, though. The toys
started to run away, but Lotso grabbed Woody's legs!
"C'mon!" Jessie tried to save Woody.

It was no use. The garbage truck arrived. All the toys were emptied into a trash compactor!

Luckily, everyone was all right.

"Where are we now?" Buzz had hit his head when he landed. Now he was back to normal.

At the dump, the toys were headed toward a trash shredder!
Buzz spotted a magnet overhead. "Grab something metal!"
Soon the magnet had pulled the toys upward.
Then Woody heard Lotso call out. "I'm stuck! Help, please!"
Woody and Buzz rescued him, and the toys moved over the
shredder onto a conveyor belt.

The toys were still in danger. Lotso was the only one who could push the STOP button and save them.

"Where's your kid now, sheriff?" Lotso walked away. He hadn't changed.

Andy's toys held hands and closed their eyes.

Suddenly, something lifted them up. The Aliens had saved them with a crane! "The Clawwwww!"

The crane left the toys near a garbage truck that looked familiar. It was the one that went by Andy's house!

Jessie grabbed Woody. "Come on! We gotta go home!"

Andy was packing his car when the garbage truck arrived. The toys snuck up to his room.

Inside, Andy's toys climbed into a box labeled ATTIC.
Woody was going to college with Andy.
Buzz reached out and shook Woody's hand.
"You know where to find us, cowboy."

Attic

Buzz jumped into the box with the other toys. Woody realized he didn't want to say good-bye to his friends. He wrote something new on the ATTIC box.

On the way to college, Andy stopped at Bonnie's house. Woody had written her address on the ATTIC box. Andy showed her the toys. "I'm going away now, so I need someone really special to play with them." He was surprised that Woody was in the box.

"My cowboy!" Bonnie gave him a giant hug.

Woody and the other toys watched Andy drive away.

"So long, partner."

Woody would miss Andy, but he would always remember the years they had spent together. Now he and the other toys had lots of new adventures with Bonnie to look forward to.